Presented to:

_____

With love from:

_____

On:

_____

*To the belief that youth does not
have to be wasted on the young.*
–LD

*To the hope that the world's girls will create
the world of their dreams.*
–MT

For Ffion
–LF

ZONDERKIDZ

Girls of the World
Copyright © 2024 by Linsey Davis
Illustrations © 2024 by Lucy Fleming

Requests for information should be addressed to:
customercare@harpercollins.com

Zondervan, *Grand Rapids, Michigan*

Hardcover ISBN 978-0-310-74966-0
Ebook ISBN 978-0-310-74972-1

Library of Congress Cataloging-in-Publication Data

Names: Davis, Linsey, author. | Tyler, Michael, 1960- author. | Fleming,
Lucy, illustrator.
Title: Girls of the world : doing more than ever before / by Linsey Davis
and Michael Tyler ; [illustrations by] Lucy Fleming.
Description: Grand Rapids : Zonderkidz, [2024] | Audience: Ages 4-8. |
Summary: Rhyming text encourages girls to join together in speaking up
for themselves to achieve their dreams and care for the earth.
Identifiers: LCCN 2022034844 (print) | LCCN 2022034845 (ebook) | ISBN
9780310749660 (hardcover) | ISBN 9780310749721 (ebook)
Subjects: CYAC: Stories in rhyme. | Girls--Fiction. |
Self-realization--Fiction. | Social change--Fiction. | LCGFT: Stories in
rhyme. | Picture books.
Classification: LCC PZ8.3.D2895 Gi 2024 (print) | LCC PZ8.3.D2895 (ebook)
| DDC [E]--dc23
LC record available at https://lccn.loc.gov/2022034844
LC ebook record available at https://lccn.loc.gov/202203484

Editor: *Megan Dobson*
Design and art direction: *Cindy Davis*

Printed in Malaysia

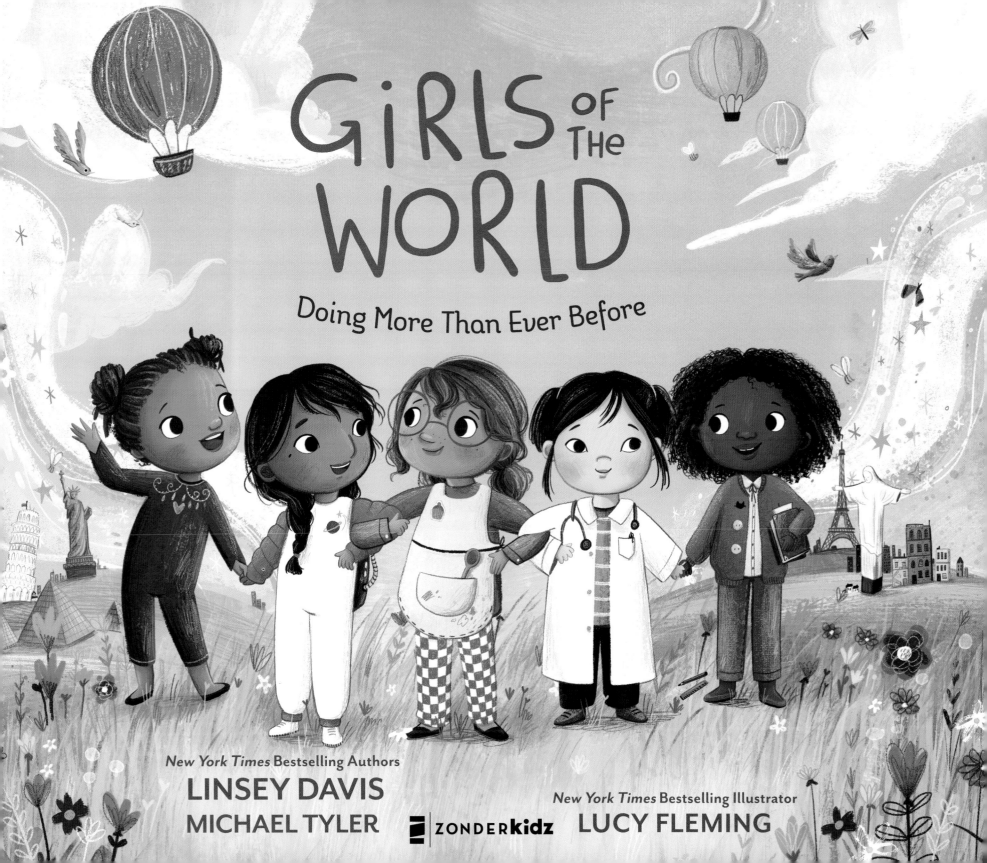

GIRLS OF THE WORLD

Doing More Than Ever Before

New York Times Bestselling Authors

LINSEY DAVIS

MICHAEL TYLER

ZONDERkidz

New York Times Bestselling Illustrator

LUCY FLEMING

The sun will shine and the moon will glow.
The birds will fly and the wind will blow.

There's another great truth all people should know.
The girls of the world are ready to go!

There are many who've gone before us,
Brave of heart and strong of mind,
Who worked so hard for justice
For girls of every kind.

They said what they could say
And did what they could do
With hopes to see the day—
When we are equal too.

It's time to urge all to follow and lead.

Let's lift up our hopes
and share what we need.

You can't stop us now that our time has come.

We're ready! Let's go—there's a lot to be done.

It's time to make real what we feel in our hearts.

Let's make our dreams matter. Each day we will start.

It's time that we get all the knowledge we crave.

Let's act with our courage and prove we are brave.

It's time we leap higher, in life's great big dance.

Let's soar to the music and cheer each advance.

It's time to be heard by the world through our voices. Speak up for ourselves and express our choices.

It's time we all work to care for our Earth. Let's guard our great planet and honor its worth.

It's time to run fast, jump high, and have fun. Let's "Hooray!" the heroes that we will become.

It's time to imagine, invent, and create.
Let's reach for the stars. Let's go beyond great.

It's time to stand up for the way that we feel.

Our dreams are our future. We'll make them all real.

It's time to make right all the things that are wrong ...

Let's face fears together. Hand-in-hand we are strong.

Let this be the day all girls become one.
Pledging to do what needs to be done.

Let's show the whole world we are fast on our way.
This is our moment. Today is the day!

To all the girls of the world,

"I'd rather regret the risks that didn't work out than the chances I didn't take at all." That heartfelt sentiment from Simone Biles underscores how our attitude can help determine our ability to achieve. I hope you are not only inspired but empowered by the successes in all shades, sizes, and ages of the girls and women who have gone before us and surround us now.

To those who once said, "You throw like a girl!" and meant it as an insult, let Mo'ne Davis, who dominated Little League baseball as a pitcher, be your example. As a little girl, I remember being so impressed, glued to the TV screen watching Debi Thomas ice-skate on the world stage at the Olympics. She was victorious in a sport in which it was so uncommon for women of color to even participate. I didn't desire to be an ice skater, but it certainly opened my eyes to what was possible—to the idea that a young, black girl like I was at that time, could and should shoot for the stars in whatever field or arena my heart desired.

I must give a personal and special thank you to Carole Simpson, who was repeatedly told she couldn't, yet she navigated her way to the highest heights of TV news as the first black woman to anchor any major newscast. She refused to allow her potential for greatness to be extinguished by the word "NO." In fact, she once told me she was fueled by all the nos. By trusting herself, pursuing her passion, and having the "audacity" to step over the obstacles and stay the course, she carved her own path all the way to the top.

Let us all follow Carole's instincts and show the world just what we can do. And so with one hand, I salute those pioneers who blazed a trail before us, and with the other I beckon you to step forward and chase your wildest and greatest dreams.

Oprah Winfrey may have said it best: "You don't become what you want; you become what you believe."

With love and belief in you,
Linsey